I0652722

Renting Superman

poetry by
Robert A. Geise

Renting Superman
Copyright ©2019 Robert A. Geise
Cover photo by: Timothy James Kinsley

All rights reserved. Blue Jade Press, LLC retains the right
to reprint this book. Permission to reprint poems from this
collection must be obtained by the author.

ISBN- 978-1-7333822-1-2

Published by:

Blue Jade Press, LLC
Vineland, NJ
www.bluejadepress.com

For Remi

Appreciation

Thanks to Barbara Brenner and Christopher Ney. Without you, I would not be the poet I am today.

Hugs and kisses to Chris M. LaBree of 2255 Productions. You've been one of my biggest cheerleaders over the years and continue to be a welcome voice of reason in my life.

Thank you to Judd Winick for teaching me, all those years ago, that if I don't sell myself, no one else will.

Thanks to Michael for recognizing the voice before I even knew I had one.

Many thanks to Mary for her technical skills.

Thanks to my brother Gordon for being such an excellent writer himself and so much to aspire to. And thanks to Paul for your unconditional love.

Thanks to Ryan and Kris. Love you, bubbas.

Acknowledgments

"Divine" appeared on Dreamland (dreamlandnews.com), 2008.

"The First Time I Bought Porn" and "Intervention" appeared in Sightlines 2007.

"Free" appeared in *Disorder*, Volume III, Summer 2017, Red Dashboard LLC Publications.

"Proof of Life" appeared in *Sightlines* 2006.

"Touching the Hornet's Nest Under a Slide by the Neighbor's Pool" appeared in Fractal Magazine, Volume II, Issue I, 2014.

Contents

every demon singing on a stage
every hu-mon earning living wage
every oozing insect in a cage
every vapid poem on the page
every mutant cell that reeks of phage
every sot who thinks he's fucking sage
every need we fearfully assuage
only leaves me eloquent with rage

Romanticizing Sebastian

The Patron Saints of Sodomites,
naked,
pierced,
broken,
beautiful.
His chest sleek, glistening,
skin prickling,
nipples hard.
In icons,
he and the tree
to which he is bound
are carved as one,
a new species
in a biblical forest.
Cypress, Sequoia
and Sebastian...
blood for sap,
branches of arrows,
pain his only fruit

Adagio

Steve enters to security beeps
and shuffles past the counter,
shelves of rubber,
skin, and expletives,
and steps into the darkness.
He joins the dance men do
in these partitioned halls,
the numbered rooms
lit by strobing exit signs
and recessed ceiling spots
dim enough to blur the deepest creases on their faces
in hopes some beautiful boy
will offer reverence
and an ass
for the length of a few dollar bills.

Steve stands with attitude
in the far corner,
ignoring signals from the stoic beerbelly,
the ruddy red cap already stroking through his jeans by
 Booth 10.
The whiff of bleach he gets from the floor
reminds him he needs to hit the Costco
on the way home
for adult diapers,
cleansing wipes,
and tubs of plain yogurt.
The thought of cultured milk and Clorox
nauseates him briefly,
but he wonders if she'd even notice it.
"This tastes funny, Stevie."
"It's fine, Mother,"
as he scoops another spoonful into her mouth.

How long will this take?
He doesn't have to wonder
as a hot blond cruises in
and looks him dead in the eye
before heading into 12
and leaving the door ajar.

Steve knows the next step..

Smolder

Whistling siren.
I am standing
inexplicably
beside burning bed.
The door is there.
I am there.
It is cold to touch.
I suddenly choke
and have a nagging urge
to claw at my eyes.
Stay and die.
Excruciating pain, then numbness,
euphoria.
Open the door and explode in a backdraft.
The lady or the tiger,
only not.
Dive into bed,
into his body,
smoldering skin,
flesh hot enough to meld.
I do.

After Aunt M.

The house is static
as we enter,
inscrutably silent.
Cuckoo clock motionless,
its pine cone weights hang low,
teardrops frozen inches from the hardwood.
Shadows grow long across the parlor floor,
cast off ceramic figurines and brass frames of family
    photos,
faces just a bit more yellowed
in this evening space.
I have never lived here.

You plod to your room
dragging the hump of your back behind you
and shut the door.
I hear you muffled through the walls
crying out the loss of lifetimes.
Your mother's death hadn't warranted such emotion.
Across the hall,
the machines are still.
Oxygen no longer hisses,
ECG doesn't beep,
even the television is blank
after countless months
of games shows and Turner Classic Movies.
Tomorrow morning,
a strong man in coveralls
will come to dismantle the bed
and remove the tanks.
"I'm very sorry for your loss," he will say.

After you wash away the 911 call,
the siren rush to the ER,
the doctor's cold condolences,
you emerge pale but levelheaded.
I cook a dinner neither of us eats
as you make the required phone calls.
Later, while you take forever
picking a shroud from
a closet full of dresses
that hadn't been worn for years,
decades, perhaps,
I crash on the couch
that smells vaguely of farina and sour milk.

It's after eleven
when you pat my head
to tell me the guest room is made.
I ask, because I think I should,
if I should sleep in your bed tonight,
but you just smile and mouth the word "no."
Instead,
before exhaustion completely sets in,
we sit holding hands at the kitchen table
waiting for a cup of chamomile,
the kettle close to seething on the stove.
You don't talk about it,
and I don't make you.
It's quiet, but not uncomfortably so.

The First Time I Bought Porn

I marched right up to the counter
and said, "*Inches*, please."

The Berlin Auction was a seedy shopping plaza
in a seedy neighborhood,
with a flea market on Sundays
and the inescapable stench of the clam bar
at the far end.
But it had good junk,
which was important to Dad
who hoarded his funds
until just the right junk presented:
another pocketknife;
a set of useless tray tables
to replace the same useless set
he got the year before;
a dozen more golf balls
even though he didn't play.
I usually wandered off
about the same time
Dad started scoping out drill bits
in the first of five hardware stores.

Dumbfounded by the kid in front of him
so deftly announcing his fagdom,
the guy at the newsstand widened his eyes
and, in exchange for four bucks,
slipped the skin mag
into a brown bag
without questioning my age.
(I was fifteen.)
The forbidden booty slid nicely
between a couple of 12" LPs
from Howard and Mann's.

I popped a boner
in the back seat
on the way home,
anticipating the orgasm I'd have
by page twelve.

Dad never asked me what I bought.

Answer?

I love to listen to Beethoven.
Among the notes is sanity, I feel.
I'm trapped within a web I've woven.

The last girl I was with was bovine.
I think if I had sliced her, I'd taste veal.
I love to listen to Beethoven.

I bought her jewels, perfume, sex, clothing
and took them all for myself – what a deal!
I'm trapped within a web I've woven.

I threw that dinner back into the oven
because she burned it black! I must appeal.
I love to listen to Beethoven.

Her virtue has yet to be proven.
But then again, I'm subject to her zeal.
I'm trapped within a web I've woven.

I need another dish to throw then...
I do not know if this or she is real.
I love to listen to Beethoven.
I'm trapped within a web I've woven.

The Day I Lied About a Lawn Chair

My mother's beehive had deflated from going in the deep
   end,
and Dad squinted without his glasses
as he talked shop to his brothers-in-law.
"That chair's broken," I told my cousins Charlene and
   Debbie.
I said the same to Aunt Grace
when she tried to sit next to me with her can of Shop Rite
 cola
and a paper plate tipping with meat from Poppop's grill.
My thirteen year-old heart sputtered, though,
when my sister's boyfriend Steve,
smooth and muscular and almost 20,
surfaced and pulled himself out of the pool in front of
   me.
I threw him my unused towel and said,
"Steve, come sit over here."
He did.

Aubade

Throwing the sheet aside,
I roll myself out of bed
and stumble toward the bath.
The air feels especially cool against
the reddened indentations on my backside.
They sting as I run my hands along the skin
and I get hard again
before I get to the toilet
and sit down, carefully.
I can't pee.
I shake my head.
Morning is just now spilling through slats
in the bathroom blinds,
and a thin bar of the stuff
shows through the open doorway
into the bed I just left
and lies across your neck and shoulders.
The cuckoo chirps six times
from down the hall,
and I sit another minute or two
trying to think about my car payment
and the electric bill
before I get the stream going.
I watch as your form morphs in the dim light,
coming closer,
until you're standing in the doorway,
crossed by sunrays
that draw to your golden skin
as if they know how often you tan.
"You're wild," you say, crossing one foot behind you
and tapping your toe on the threshold between rooms.
"You know what I like," I lie a little.

You didn't know to spit in my face
while I went down on you,
and you didn't know not to call me pussy-boy.
"Thank you," you reply
and step to me,
hugging my head into your stomach,
stretching your hands and arms down my back.
"Thanks for a great night," I say.
You know it's a dismissal and step back from me.
"I don't want to go yet," you whisper.
I stand and suddenly realize
you're not as tall as you seemed
when you were standing over me
giving orders or filling holes.
This time, I give the orders
as I walk past you
to gather your clothes
from the bedroom.

Ice Cream
(the poem formerly known as "Treat")

It was my twenty-minute lunch hour
from my seven-day job at Tommy's Seaside,
Atlantic City, mid-July.
The boardwalk bustled
with anxious gamblers,
tons of kids in bathing suits,
and sun-baked tourists.
Not really hungry,
but I had a sweet tooth.
The Baskin-Robbins
run by Pakistanis
wasn't too busy despite the heat.
"Thank you, Sir, please come again!"
I just wanted a single dip of
chocolate chip cookie dough
in a sugar cone
and I didn't care that it would melt
in the haze
and the humid afternoon air.

Sweat beaded on my brow
as I waited in line for my treat.
Then I found one ahead of me —
a tall, toned and tan lifeguard
in a tank and red Speedos
leaned his brown body against the window
and asked for a triple-scoop sundae,
extra whipped cream,
crushed Oreos,
cherries, bananas, wet nuts.

That could only make him sweeter, I thought
giving him the once-over
from the thick thatch of impossibly black hair
to his enormous bare feet
which shuffled thoughtlessly.
The soles were peppered
with sand from the beach,
debris from the boards,
even some ABC gum, I think.

I stared quite consciously
at those big, brown, dirty feet.
I wondered what it meant
that all I could think about
was licking them clean
while he's on his back,
legs in the air
as I plow his tan-lined ass,
hearing him scream in ecstasy:
"Thank you, Sir, please come again!"

Casually adjusting myself,
I stepped out of line
and headed back to work.
Ice cream wasn't gonna cut it.

Death to *Moby Dick*
(after the 1956 film directed by John Huston)

Consent not to her magnetism;
allow it to abate unquelled.
Resist Saint Elmo's Fire
and the rush of the open ocean's fury
as passion's curse pumping
through the chambered nautilus
of Ahab's Hell heart.

The savage allures as pyrite,
and God's own puppet will dance
on the pulpit in vain.
Smell not land on open water
and save the crew from lunatic portents.
Allow them pleasures of the flesh,
women of easy virtue.
Allow them to eat of ambrosia and caviar.
Allow them to age beyond the expectancy
of the white whale's sea.
Allow them to die drowned,
their last moments
the most ecstatic,
most satisfying of their lives.

Underwater

I first see
Creature from the Black Lagoon,
a black and white horror
on a color television
one Saturday afternoon.
I'm maybe ten?
It's Mom's time for food shopping with Grandmom
and Dad's time to do whatever he did
when he wasn't around.
And my brother babysits me from
the comfort of his bedroom.
(I set the rug on fire once,
just to get his attention.)

Julie Adams might put an eye out
with those torpedo tits,
but I'm much more interested in
Richards Carlson and Denning
and how much they don't wear
through what seems like most of the film.
I imagine the creature grabbing at Adams' tiny feet
in hopes of eliminating her
and luring the Richards below
for some underwater play.
It's not bestial —
even at this young age
I'm well aware that
beneath the must-have-been-green rubber bodysuit
is another man,
naked and muscular.
He and the Richards
could reenact a scene from
an Esther Williams film,
kicking up waves and

making pretty triangles in the water
before disappearing
beneath the surface,
smiling all the way to the bottom.

Marks

One day in seventh grade,
Mike Cunningham wrapped my wrist
in the chain of a pair of nunchucks
and squeezed until it hurt.
I yelped, not completely dismayed,
but more surprised.
He released me from the metal grip
and we examined the four round close-set indentations.
The mark of the chain will be with you,
he said,
forever.
The word clung to me all day,
as did those marks,
through lunch and recess,
science and social studies.
Mr. Szigethy's denims
seemed tighter that day,
and wasn't his shirt unbuttoned an extra button?

On the bus ride home,
already hard from the load welling in my groin,
I fingered the marks like Braille
and closed my eyes.
Mr. Szigethy unbuttons his shirt
the rest of the way
and drops it off his shoulders
to reveal a harness and tit clamps,
things I was just learning about
from magazines I swiped
from the back of the drugstore.
His jeans fall,
exposing a leather jock strap.

His skin is mottled with scars,
burn marks, bruises, and brandings,
head to hairy toes.
He grabs his sheathed joint,
stuffed liberally into its pouch,
and orders me in his deep,
authoritarian tone,
"Take it, boy."

Exiting the bus with my books in front of me,
I jetted from the stop
at Folsom Country Store
past mile marker 3
down Mays Landing Road,
dashed through the yard,
unlocked what I knew was an empty house,
ran up the stairs
into the bathroom,
and slammed the door shut behind me.

Waiting

As a boy I was terrified I'd run into poison ivy every time I stepped out of the house. You'll get a rash, Grandmom said, and it won't go away. It'll just get itchier and itchier. Every plant on the edge of the woods behind my house suddenly grew trifoliate with a reddish hue. I avoided the outdoors one summer entirely.

My mother warned me about tooth decay and germs of the mouth, how they'd rot my teeth if I didn't brush. I brushed and brushed, every day, first three, then four and five times a day, but it was never enough.

Joan Rivers hosted a PSA bemoaning Tay-Sachs disease and its devastating effects on children. Even though I had no idea what it was, I knew I had it and dreamed I was going to die.

Barely a teenager, I watched Beverly Williams on Eye-Witness News speak gravely of "the gay plague" and men dying in San Francisco and New York of no known cause. I hadn't even tasted a man's kiss let alone cock, yet I knew someday I would die just as they, in shame and fear. I pleasured myself nightly, secreting some of my brother's porn stash into my own room. I experimented with clothes pins, fruits and vegetables, Vicks VapoRub, all in preparation for the gay lifestyle I'd live. I needed to be good at sex so that I could please any man at any moment's notice. I'd have to squeeze in a lifetime of living into only a few years of fucking before I'd start with diarrhea, low-grade fevers, Kaposi's sarcoma, night sweats.

One weekend my parents went down the shore, I found myself nude in my bedroom with a 23-year-old man two months before my sixteenth birthday. He let me do whatever I wanted, so I did. He did it all to me in return. Then I waited.

Proof of Life

There's a documentary
on late-night cable TV
about an old man who died
alone in the world.
No living relatives,
partner long deceased,
one night as he lay sleeping,
his heart stopped, and he passed.

It was weeks before anyone noticed.

Dispassionate office workers
squared away paperwork.
A grizzled coroner
honored his final wishes
to be buried next to his family
in a pre-purchased plot.

A disposal team was sent
to clean out his apartment.
Uninterested and uncaring,
death's custodians
rifled his personal belongings,
chuckled at odd collections.
They read through diaries and yearbooks.
His senior portrait showed a handsome face
full of joy and energy.
After high school,
he must have acted on stage.
There were yellowed clippings
of shows he'd performed in,
before years of toil and drudgery
that doubtless lent
to his demise.

They emptied his refrigerator,
mayo, milk, boxed wine,
leftover Chinese.

Strangers cartoned up
what was left of his existence,
and set it out for trash.
They pulled pictures from the walls
to reveal virgin paint
that hadn't seen dust or light of day
for decades.
His furniture went to the Goodwill.

At the man's burial,
a volunteer preacher read a static, clichéd eulogy
to an audience of professional pallbearers,
men thinking of the meal waiting on the dinner table,
the episode of *CSI* they'd seen the night before,
a girlfriend's warm pussy.
They lowered the man's postage-paid casket
into the earth
and went back to their lives,
soon to forget
a name they never knew.

Sitting on a comfortable, broken-in couch,
crotchety old cat purring on the throw by my side,
my love already gone to bed hours before,
I wonder.

Free

I find myself, since your departure, free
of happiness. I turn to anything
to change my world and live in ecstasy.

I take a yoga class, do some tai chi.
With all the time, I have to do something.
I find myself, since your departure, free.

I have no appetite, so I don't eat.
For six-pack abs, I'll starve entirely
to change my world and live in ecstasy.

Coke, marijuana, crystal meth and E...
To pay for heroin, I sell your ring.
Is anything, since your departure, free?

I fuck a bunch of guys with HIV
(who pound my ass raw hanging in a sling)
to change my world and live in ecstasy.

I can't remember if you left crying
or if I left you, as you lay dying.
I find myself, since your departure, free
to change my life and live in ecstasy.

The Day My Mother, at God's Behest, Stepped into My Room

She sits on a bed,
springs creaking like memory
in a room
paneled with brown splinters
beneath posters of bands
she shouldn't have let him
listen to.

She reads of her son's sexuality
in a letter addressed to anyone but her
and cries her real tears.

Her grandchildren,
with whom she planned to begin anew,
are choked by sentences
typed into rope on a page.

Her son's beauty doesn't die,
it never existed.

She remembers him,
a charming baby in baby overalls
against a soft blue background.
Trying to coax a smile,
she dangled keys in front of him
to stop his crying.
His eyes sparkled
at the rainbow trout keychain
that fluoresced blue and green,
sometimes purple.
He looked up,
his mouth wide in awe,
and was blinded by the flash.

Intervention
(thanks to Eoin Kinnarney)

It's a breath
choked hard on cheap cologne,
blood drops
brown and cold
beside broken glass
on faded tile floor,
a cataract
turned milk's gray from stillborn blue,
some jackass dancing nude
through the gold and scarlet street
of a Bollywood bazaar.

Detach with love,
I am ordered
by deluded succubae
whose sex is so stagnant,
their ovaries are already cremains.
I cannot.
They recite the Lord's Prayer.
I cannot.

Flopped on the sofa
in a house of nice
surrounded by his American dreams,
he metabolizes poison
unconscious.
Again.

Too weary to even weep,
I kiss the toad on the forehead,
lift the keys, let them jangle,
and pull the door shut behind me.
A haloed moon shines white

through a marble ceiling of clouds.
Starting up,
I shift into first,
point the car toward the Atlantic,
and tempt Triton's fate.

After Pulse

Bané is in from Cali
for a work thing
so I grab the husband
and head to dinner
on South Street in Philly.
It's easily twenty years
since I held him,
but he feels the same
when we meet up
at Loews on Market.
Uber to Jon's Grille,
decide the evening is al-fresco worthy.
I face the street
and expect the usual show
though I'm distracted
by the guy a table over
playing with his bare feet
which he's displaying like a prize.
"All of this could be yours!"
I concentrate on Bané's accent
or lack thereof
since last we spoke.
I still hear the Serb,
a boy barely a man
immersed in American culture
as a lobster to the seething pot.
It's in his voice
when he introduces Orlando
and forty-nine dead,
the disdain, the disquiet.
He fled the bullets
of the Yugoslav Wars
but wonders when
a round from an AR-15

will split his aorta
or separate vertebrae in his spine
as he stops for cilantro at the grocery
on his way home from a business meeting.
Maybe the Brown Motor Works,
bringing the chopper in
for scheduled service
since it's still under warranty.
The church he attends
with Kristine's family,
genuflecting to a giant crucifix,
appropriately bloody
as He watches this flock liberated
by a camouflage revenant,
also one of His own.
Bané falls across his in-laws,
not a hero but a statistic,
and hollers for his wife
to play dead
with his death rattle.
She hears his Serbian,
and wonders what he means
with her last thought.

Myq & T

His touch is adrenaline
to the pet store garter.
It darts left, right,
lunges back away from his large hands,
then zooms up his arm
and under the sleeve of his
Dillinger T-shirt.
His monstrous form jiggles a bit
before the snake reappears
beneath his chin,
rustling the whiskers of his goatee.
He chuckles deeply,
the way he does,
and guides the serpent back to his hand.
She watches him,
this sheep in wolf's clothing,
remembers their initial meeting
at a Dracula's Ball
on Halloween Night,
a blind date
set up by a man named Fox
who told her,
"You'll love him!"
The first sight of him,
Gothic robes still short
on his mountain of a frame,
confirmed the ridiculous portent.
The evening of small talk
(that was anything but)
and some minor moshing to Rammstein
brought the evening
and her to his place.
She crept comfortably up the apartment stairs,
candles melted to each step.

Poe on the wall,
bed of nails on the floor,
more gargoyles than haunt Notre Dame.
Spotting the python behind glass,
she knew she was home.

Dating Whitman

Reading *Leaves of Grass*
and drinking white zinfandel,
I eat penne pasta at Mamma Mia's.
Erik is green at this:
the inappropriate sense of urgency,
the straight expression,
the focus on larger parties.
I don't dismay
the lack of attention.

Walt is fine company.
I pour him a glass
as I study his visage
on the sleeve.
I don't go for the beard,
but that's all right.
Walt is every man and any man.
Tonight, for me,
he's clean shaven.
His hair is jetblack sunrise,
eyes the blue of bachelor buttons.
Old and young,
my Walt is 42,
experience and advantage
yet still ready to go all night.
Towering and elfish,
he stands just shy of 6',
enough to look up a little bit
into those cornflower eyes
were we face to face.

I see his drawers
hanging on his hips,
resting on the curve of his generous ass.

He doesn't need a washboard —
the smooth, rounded gut is perfection,
broad shoulders leading to slender but taut arms.
I don't worry about his penis.
He's horse hung or not, or both, or neither.

No matter.
I tease him with Erik's tasty build and buns
and work him up sufficiently
to leave the table incarnate,
a century post-mortem.
He follows me to the men's room
where we bring each other to completion
before he's off to another table
in another restaurant
for another man
as another man.
But still mine.

Trudy's Ashes

The vet's office phoned today so I headed over. Clouds
would be cliché but also true, of course. The receptionist
handed me a small wooden box, smooth and stained
cherry. It weighed more than life. There was a card
accompanying the cremains, sympathizing and advertising
simultaneously. "Sorry your pet's dead. Tell your friends!"
My mother held the box when I got home and cried. "I
never got to say goodbye."

I couldn't say goodbye. My husband blubbered over that
tiny feline body between injections, his tears dropping on
the stainless examination table with a thup. We stroked
her skeletal form, played with her jellybean toes. We told
Doctor Matt about the day she came home with us,
weighing not much less than the tiny corpse-in-waiting.
She complained all the way home, as she had all the way
to her death that morning. It was cloudy that day, too.

In the house at 118 Main Street, I lie on the couch watching
a *Star Trek* rerun with Trudy sleeping between my knees
like an upside-down turtle, post-midnight. Her front paws
kneed the air, and her purr vibrates against my legs. Her
eyes close and open slowly. Before I join my husband
already in bed, I turn off the television and stay with her,
the two of us nodding in and out sleep. As I drift, I feel the
moment. It is now, and it is endless.

Renting Superman

Rentboy.com says you're 28,
which is years too young for me.
But your return call is prompt
and you can host
so I choose not to beg.

The GPS gives me the runaround.
When I get to the place,
you answer the door
in nothing more than plaid shorts
that hang off your hips
(as I would, in a few minutes).

The modest apartment smells vaguely of Hot Pockets.
We discuss ground rules and limits
without a hint of irony.
You offer me a bottled water.

I follow you to the bedroom
wishing you would hold my hand
but knowing it's probably a courtesy
you don't extend to tricks.

It's spotless, pedestrian —
tile floor, basic walls,
television, PC,
bed with just a fitted, no pillows.
The one splash of color
is a huge cardboard Superman
dangling off wire
from the ceiling in the corner.
Cartoon Clark is decked in his tightest tights and cape,
brilliant primary red, blue and yellow,
and the exaggerated S nearly splitting

between those freakish pecs.

Your muscles are human,
solid and perfect.
Your trunk is shaved,
balls smooth
and ready for a stranger's touch.
Behind and below, though,
a jungle of hair through which
I fight to find you.

The ad said you kiss,
but your lips lie limp
when I try to tongue your mouth,
so I give that up to focus on your cock
which responds well enough.
We take a break
when I lose my breath.

I climb off my knees
and lead you to the mirror
where I stand in back of you.
Your extended fingers pull up my thigh
as my middle-aged frame steals
a bit of self-confidence
from your bump and grind.
Your irises are gray and cool, not icy,
and I see myself for a moment
as you must see yourself every day.

Still, the look in your eyes
(or lack thereof)
when I tell you to cum on my face
makes it clear why I'm there.

My time over,

I drop two hundred
and leave you
to clean up the mess.

I don't regret
the fire in my throat
that makes me hard again in the car
and doesn't subside
until I get home
and toss another load into the trash
faster than a speeding bullet.
A gin and tonic soothes the burn
as I save your number to my contacts.

"FAGS"

The smell of burnt rubber hovers over what's left of their home. They cling to each other and the neighbors still click their tongues in agreement with the word spray painted on the sooted welcome mat. Tyler trips over the broken threshold to see if the hard drive is worth rescuing. Martin loads a chainsaw and gardening clippers into the Ford's flatbed. He collects the remaining contents of the work shed before Tyler returns empty handed, healthy pink face smudged with black ash, or maybe the bruises are finally coming out. Wired from the wane of coke, Martin chugs cans of Diet Pepsi to adjust his screaming metabolism and delivers himself into the trailer's carcass. The blood drops on the melted couch cushion are now brown and black in front of him.

They were fresh the night before, on the furniture and on his jeans, and dried into the gnarled knuckles of his right hand. Tyler emerges from behind the door that was locked and barricaded the night before, black half-moons beneath his bloodshot eyes.

"You seen my smokes?" he rasps with sandpaper vocal chords. Martin leans over, feeling his ribs acutely from the one good shot Tyler got in, and grabs the pack from beneath the IKEA lamp. He extends his arm back to Tyler, who doesn't hesitate to take the cigarettes or touch Martin's hand... Feeling its lack of weight, he says, "Where's my lighter?"

"Fuck if I know," Martin announces, still favoring his tender chest. "Use the stove if it still works."

Mother Waits

There's a paperclip on the dash,
plastic coated
red and white like a candy cane.
I cry to a toll taker labeled Mona
how I'm on my way to Cooper Medical Center,
mother in ICU,
diabetic coma,
hanging by a thread,
forgot my wallet,
don't even know if I have the gas
to make it.
"Go on, shug,"
she says waving me through.
The ride is smooth after that.

I pass Cooper.

Alan answers the door in his open robe
and nothing else.
I expect to see other boys
but we're oddly alone.
"Do what you want," I say.
I'm thrown across
the back of the couch,
jeans ripped down.
Just Shoot Me is on TV
as he begins his assault
without a drop of KY or spit,
never mind the care of a condom.
Yeah, it hurts.
It's something.

It's over in a minute,
he was so hot from waiting.
I think I yawn as he pulls out,
dripping cum and blood on the carpet beneath.
"Glass of wine?" he asks.

I've had enough wine.
I grab my keys and bolt.
Perhaps I'll go to the mall
and tell little children
there is no Santa Claus.

Benoit

Woman lies in bed,
breathing,
no longer crying.
He lies opposite,
finally quiet, settled.
They both stare blankly
through a fourth wall.

She sees his thick body
wrapped around a man.
He's always had other lovers,
men of bulging biceps,
lightning veins,
massive, gold thighs.
He holds them so close,
the lines of their flesh blur
in the violent dance.
Chest to chest,
nipples touching,
he embraces each,
looking thoughtfully
into his opponent's eyes
before the fall.

He handles them
with the love
of his life's work.
He never hurts them
intentionally.

She feels his hands
close around her throat.
She sees him
tangled in ropes,

an inverted tree of woe.
She sees their son
lifeless beneath a pillow
stained with vomit and tears.
She sees the lights dim
in an empty auditorium
as the bell rings
on a dark match.

Touching the Hornet's Nest
Under a Slide by the Neighbor's Pool

The first was a mere needle prick,
the nurse with a syringe
on flu shot day at the drug store.

The second was a real jab
like that of a green phlebotomist,
or one pissed off at his boyfriend.
"I'll slip you the injection, Steve. *There!*"

The third was a nail
fresh from the forge,
driven into flesh by a ball peen
and warmed up from sitting by the fire.

The fourth was a scalpel,
pressing into skin already numb to pain
but not sensation.
(Perhaps a worse feeling.)

I lost count after that.
I couldn't count how many times
faggot had been thrown my way
before I even set foot in high school.
I swelled inside a little more
each time my friends
(how were they friends?)
called me one for striking out again.
Then a man eighteen years my elder
let me touch him
underwater,
where I escaped the swarm of hornets
angered by my invasion
of their personal wasp space

the summer before.
His liquid stung my throat,
and I exploded.

The Transparent Self

Contemplating the lost language of the crane,
I embrace my heartbeat, the gain
and loss of my lungs. My health,
like me, is invisible, skilled in stealth.
Pills, sleep, dementia, and, of course, the pain.

I'd swallow it all, even feign
joy, would any I have known as *friend* deign
to come see this transparent self
and speak to me the lost language of the crane.

They do not. Their T-cells remain
intact; therefore, the only strain
they feel is shoulders beneath shelves
on which they accumulate things and wealth.
No, I disappear without so much as a stain
left to indicate the lost language of the crane.

Children at Play

My sister does not wear the dress
so much as it wears her —
a second skin
it's on her so often.
Mother introduces her
as "Sara and her dress"
to the next future ex-husband
whose name is more that of a race horse
than a man who made his money
off sub-prime mortgage loans
and got out before the crash.
"That's a pretty dress,"
he sings condescendingly.
"They'll bury me in it,"
my sister predicts,
"after I defenestrate myself."
Mother's eyes close slowly,
her face flushing again.
"Wherever did you learn such a word??"
though she knows full well
where the accountant sends the checks.
"Follow me, love," I say
tugging at her arm toward the kitchen.
"We'll start the trepanation immediately."
"And soil my pretty dress??" she begs.
"Perish the thought."
Next Future Ex-Husband is aghast.
Mother giggles a little too loudly
to break the tension
as Sara and I skip away,
froufrou from her dress
echoing defiance.

Shopping

Half my age,
a young man in a yellow-green vest
limps through the market lot
mating carts,
corralling them along the store front.
Giant red letters announce
"CHICKEN BREAST $1.99/lb."

I press my nose
to the glass door
before it notices me.

The air between
produce and dairy
is solid with cold.
It stunts my breath
with its closeness.

I find frozen foods
more claustrophobic
than the pair of purple denims
of some ungodly waist size
that haunted my walk-in
two years short of twenty.
They were buttoned for moments
until I peeled them off
and tossed them in a pile
for Goodwill.

They're adopted by a blond boy,
perfect skin and curves,
not ignorant of his gorgeous youth.
He knows every line in *The Breakfast Club*,
every note of Bronski Beat.

His Christian parents sleep soundly,
confident he's not
slipping out of jeans
for strange men in parked cars.

David's Hand

I see him sitting
in the book store café
where I read pretty poetry
at the censored open mic
Third Thursday every month.
His ruddy brow and redhead hairline
betray his years,
as unloved love handles do my own,
and his body is long and slender,
narrow shoulders,
hidden hips and ass.
(I always look.)
Feigning sensitivity
to the light pouring in from the autumn afternoon,
I excuse myself into his table,
the single shady spot in the place.
"Sure," he says smoothly,
meeting my gaze.
"I'm David."
The blue in his eyes is new to me,
as if I've lived my entire life
and never noticed the color of the sky until this moment.

He's writing code on a Dell Inspiron,
15" monitor,
sleek ruby skin.
"Try it out," he offers
and spins the piece to face me.
His voice is as comfortable
as the smooth keyboard beneath my fingers.
I type, "welcome to my world,"
beneath the blanket of foreign language
before surrendering the device
back to his talented typing.

We small talk about servers, proxies,
paginators.
He uses words like *obtuse* and *iconoclast*
as easily as he sips his coffee,
just a few shades of brown darker than cream
and smelling vaguely of hazelnut.
He doesn't need background when I propose
the Flying Spaghetti Monster
and order him to obey his Noodly Master.
He chuckles, in fact,
in a deep tenor that
reveals his first smile to me.
We laugh together
before a benign pause
completed by the faint refrain
of Tracey's *New Beginning* on the overhead
and the tail end of a latte's whoosh.

Ignoring my presence momentarily
to review a few kernels of data,
he lays his left arm on the table
alongside the laptop.
His hand, slender fingers, thick thumb,
and trimmed nails, extends slightly,
open far enough
to offer invitation.

Do I take it?
Do I place the fingers of my damaged right hand
into his
and wait for response?

Will he close his grasp tightly
like Venus's flytrap
in an unspoken admission
that he was pleased as I

to have met a man
in a public place
with a private intelligence
too difficult to explain
to anyone but another
who understands?
Will he take my hand lightly,
casually,
indicate an ambivalence toward connecting
with another person,
another man
or connecting with me?
Will he withdraw it slowly,
surprise in those unreal blue eyes
with a look begging for explanation beyond apology
but allowing silence instead?
Will he pull it away quickly,
furrow that ruddy brow
and say, "What the fuck, man?"

My fingers tremble,
inches from his.

Part of me wants him to take my hand,
stand me up and spin me around,
like a scene from a Fred and Ginger film
and dance among readers,
caffeine addicts, and hipsters,
extras oblivious to our unexpected choreography.
Part of me wants him to give my hand a squeeze,
let it go,
and get up with a sidelong glance
that begs following
through the stacks
and into the public restroom
where he locks the door behind us,

rips down my jeans,
and takes me from behind
with his saliva as my only protection.
Part of me wants him to hold my hand until evening,
until the employees politely kick us out,
and lead me to his car,
something modest, functional and clean.
He wants to know how I feel
about impulsiveness.
"Can you disappear for a few days?"
he asks sweetly,
eyes glowing green
beneath the streetlight
diffused by moist and chilling air.

His hand drops
as I confess.

At Brokeback's Peak

I stare down the western edge
anticipating its daggered rocks
and unforgiving granite slope
to the flat plain,
green as God's beard
flowing fan-like outward
to the end of the earth,
the curve of my lover's back and body
prone on the horizon,
so far from me.
My Ennis waits
at the edge of the mountain,
this breaker of men
as much as I.
Yet he is no more mine
than the death
I can't bring myself to
before I step back
and think of his hair
between my fingers,
his tongue on my lip,
his navel pressed to mine
again.

Aubade 2

My head wills itself to rise
despite a brain asleep.
Eyes open to swirling movement,
the only sound a light rain
falling over a circle of grass.
In the first morning light
through heavy, coal-colored clouds,
the forest is a planetary,
cosmic thing.

Then, I remember

and raise myself to my elbows
to spy your beautiful form
just out of reach.
The undersides of your legs
race to the perfect curve of your ass
that in turn swoops to your back,
droplets of rain beading there
on the finest of hairs.
Your face is benign,
untwisted despite the righteous fucking
that left us depleted hours earlier
and tumbling to the ground for respite.
Your lips are parted so
and gloss from the rain
mixed with our voracity.
I can smell your last load
on my breath.

I sit up, hard.
I think I'd like to hold you in my arms.
Yet I don't know your name
or much else,

and I am sure all you know of me
is how I feel from the inside.
I watch you sleep.

Rain retreating to a fine mist,
I stand flaccid
(already reading too much into it)
and slowly pull on a pair of pants
I think are mine.
Precipitation dwindles to nothing
as I see your undiminished beauty.
Before I turn away,
the clouds part quite suddenly
and bathe your face and body in sunlight
the color of butternut squash.
Your brow furrows from the intrusion.
Your eyes, still closed, scrunch
as you lift your head and turn away,
settling back into sleep
without a word or even a moan.
I don't look back
as I head toward what might be
the direction of my car
and wonder why I covet escape so desperately.

Crime Scene

Looking through the glass darkly,
she absorbs the midnight scene,
numb to the red and blue strobe.
Drizzle blurs the initial observation,
drops zigzagging past her sightline
into nonexistence.
She fingers her shield thoughtlessly.
The boys are hovering,
waiting for a late coroner.
She notices Mags' foot
pressing the corner of the sheet
flat to the shining pavement
as the breeze tickles the cloth
away from the crime.
A glimpse of pink,
then nothing.
She caresses the door handle,
smooth and cool.
The skin of her lover's arm.
She throws back the sheet
and sees a woman like herself:
strong, black, glistening.
Which part will I use this tongue on first?
Her lover giggles as she digs into the pink.

Divine

The girl can't help it.
She wraps a size-14 green satin frock
around her size-18 curves,
slips on her favorite cha-cha heels
and heads down to the Corvettes
to do her shopping.
Bleach blond bouffant
still smelling of Aqua Net,
penciled half-moon eyebrows
over emerald shadow to match her outfit
and maraschino cherry red lipstick,
she sashays down the aisle
between HABA and housewares
as if on the runway in New York,
Milano,
Paris.
It's not until electronics
that she makes eye contact
with any of the myriad gawkers,
terrified employees hiding behind endcaps,
mortified mothers pulling their pointing brats
into their polyester stretch pants,
men in stained white tank tops
eyes and crotches bulging.
She smiles joker-like
and flicks her tongue
to greet the blue-haired granny,
whose jaw falls to her hand-crocheted lace collar.
In hardware, she winks
at the little colored girl
pretty in a pink dress
before she clears the path
between men's and women's,
walks straight past the checkout counters

and right out the automatic doors
with a 20" Magnavox under one arm
and a Dolmar chainsaw cradled in the other.
It doesn't matter where she's going or why,
she just is.

Exhibit A

I was probably eight, maybe nine
when one night at dinner
I asked my parents directly,
"What's pornography?"
I might have read it somewhere —
I'd just started straying away from the children's section
at the library.
Mom and Dad looked at each other
and registered no emotion that I recognized
at the time.
Dad continued shoveling in potatoes
as my mother said,
"It's pictures of men and women with no clothes on."
And that's all that was said,
aside from my little brother asking,
"Can I have the last pork chop?"

A couple three months later,
at Nan and Pap's,
I got a gander at my first *National Geographic*.
As I glanced at the glossy pages,
I asked Nan,
"Is this pornography?"
She nearly dropped her feather duster in the aquarium
but recovered quickly.
"Heavens, no!" she informed me.
"It's nature! Natural!"
That had to be good, right?
PBS aired a program called *Nature*
and we watched that all the time!

In the magazine there were many natural photos,
dozens of shots of brown women
muddied or adorned with metal hoops and rings,

their sagging breasts unfettered
and naked babies, all bulbous heads and bellies,
 at their feet.
Natural, but I was mostly bored
until I turned to pages of California surfers.
Ruddy men in tiny briefs soaked with salt water.
Sun bleached blond boys riding boards on huge swells.
Nude men poorly lit by the dusk
as they showered on a private beach.
Was that a peepee in that picture?
I stared awfully hard.
I wondered what it would be like
to stand outside of a building,
outside of a *bathroom*
without a towel,
without a pair of tighty whiteys
to hide my privates.
I shivered head to toe, in fact,
at the thought of a camera spotting me
wet and dressed in just my skin
while standing near the ocean.
I knew it was something I wanted to try,
wanted to be.

The Criminal

I wanted him,
so I stole him.

I stole his friendship
with those same antiquated clichés.

I stole his trust
by telling him what he wanted to hear.

I stole his love,
and along with it,
hers.

I stole his semen,
as if only to prove that I could,
and in so doing,
I stole his self-respect.

I stole his family,
though they were through with him.
After me, anyway.

I stole his friends.
I stole his money.

I stole his laugh.
I stole his vanity.
I stole his favorite things.

I stole his hands, his hair.
I stole his smile.

I stole everything from him
and once I had,

I gave it all back to him,
wrapped in a package
of deceit and disappointment.

Because once I stole everything from him,
I didn't want him anymore.

And what I can't figure out
is how many times
I can possibly steal him
without stealing myself.

Love Beeps
(after "Physics" by Peter E. Murphy)

Peter says everything beeps.
Rather, Peter says every beeping thing

moves us apart little by little in the inertia
of the expansion of the universe.

Even beeping love. Love beeps? Perhaps.
But once the universe can expand no farther,

it will collapse just as slowly, bringing
every beeping thing closer together.

Even beeping us, Peter.
Even beeping us.

Horror Movies

I am 15.
It's a dark room
with rustic brown paneling
and a toilet bowl blue rug.
Eurythmics and Thompson Twins
shed a bit of light,
but overall,
it's still dark.
Unmade bed with unwashed sheets,
I lie on my stomach,
arms hanging over the end
and watch a Saturday night horror film that wasn't scary
when released fifteen years before.
The Conqueror Worm has nothing to do
with the Poe poem I read
because I liked to read,
but Vincent Price always livened up any show.
Eventually I drift off
and wake Sunday morning,
television turned off by a parent
wandering in the room
to snoop without actually snooping.

I am 19.
The sky is black
because it's about ten p.m.
and there are clouds but no rain.
I'm parked in the Rabbit,
watching the tail end of *Little Shop of Horrors*
at Atco Drive-In.
I've littered the passenger bucket seat
with Reese's Pieces and Doritos,
and I'm sipping on generic root beer.
Audrey II explodes,

and "Don't Feed the Plants" has no place
in this Hollywood ending.
Credits roll, and the screen is blank briefly.
Previews and advertisements,
then *The Witches of Eastwick*.
Michelle, Susan, Cher.
I'm in gayboy heaven.

I am 22.
I can't stand straight in this room
for the short ceiling
so it's set up as a TV room,
pillows and cushions for comfort.
Boyfriend went to bed an hour ago,
put off by another viewing of *Twilight Zone: The Movie*.
I pop in a brand new find from Sam Goody at the mall,
a childhood favorite,
Halloween with the (New) Addams Family.
I remember some of the bits,
hopping egg hors d'oeurves,
the ol' piccolo trick,
and Mother Frump's pterodactyl demise.
The kooky family singing
"A Merry, Creepy Halloween" triggers an unexpected tear.
As the tape ends,
the VCR powers off,
the TV full of sudden snow.

I am 34.
He's passed out again,
no "good night" before staggering upstairs.
I pop the DVD out of the case,
slip it in the tray,
and watch it disappear.
Some preliminary crap
leads to the main menu,

and I press play.
John Carpenter's The Thing.
Kurt Russell is searing
despite the horizon of snow
and the chilling story.
I haven't watched this in forever
and I love that it's nearly new.

I am 47.
It's almost Halloween night.
Husband and mother-out-law drove down to Myrtle Beach
to escape New Jersey
and an unexpected early winter
for a few days.
Night of the Creeps on Blu-ray.
I watch with commentary
(both tracks),
all the special features,
original and alternative endings.
Cats sleep in spots,
ears twitching infrequently from the Surround.
I'm warm in sweats
and clutching pillows
on about a third of the couch.

I am 62.
I napped when I got home
so I'd make it through the evening.
I've already queued up some classics on Amazon
and start *Children Shouldn't Play with Dead Things*
to get me in the spirit.
I finish *Shaun of the Dead* for the fortieth time,
and the show continues.
James from work and his wife are a no-show,
and it's not until halfway through *It Follows*
that I get the alert.

"Cant make it sorry thanks again see you monday".
He could have called,
but it's okay.
I click off after that,
forsaking *Nightmare on Elm Street 2*,
and head to bed,
reciting silent good nights in my head.

Unsurprised

I'm not surprised
when your cheeks go red,
face flushing with
the same blood
that hardens your cock
in your jeans
as you press against me
while we French kiss in your office
on a Sunday.
Our husbands are home,
or wherever,
doing what our husbands do
while we're off not doing
what we're supposed to.

We torment each other
with tales of the men our lives cling to.
Sitting on the couch again,
dinner unmade,
dishes filling the sink.
The snoring.
Fifteen years spent in New Jersey
over ten promised
in Florida or Arizona.
Plucking bathroom tissue
from the crack of his fattened ass
at his behest.

I ask why we don't run off,
live happily for a while,
no expectation of "ever after."
We'd just be us
somewhere that would want us to be.

The disarming smile
tells me you blush
because you've already thought
these same thoughts
a thousand times
before you masturbated, and after,
to thoughts of me
still pressing that hardness against mine
not to fruition,
but anticipation.

I tell you not to answer.

Lake Gordon

Though the breeze is chilling, almost autumnal, the mid-May air more than hints of water lily native to this mereside. No sun is apparent, but I walk a bright path, worn by uncountable footfalls, and hug tightly the fulgent water's edge. It's always water we cling to in life, or that clings to us in death, in kidney failure.

Reeds and weeds stand tall, short, and tall again. A Canada goose preps her brood, hissing in fear and craning their tiny necks, for quick escape into the drink. With a wave of his great wing, the gander disarms his family, and they quiet, going about their goose business. If only all fathers qualified for such respect from their children.

I cross a careworn wooden bridge to a tall islet and ascend its incline to the peak. Surrounded by swamp maple, only now do I hear the sigh of the water's static change.

I focus on Lake Gordon, its influenced surface. Still, I only see him, dying of Amyloidosis on Saint Lambert's Day eight months ago. When my mother suffered him to let his body die, he said, I know. He wouldn't look at me.

It's clearly time to go. The lake is grey and smells of sulfur.

Trout

I stood behind the boy
in the bank today,
though he wasn't a boy
because he cashed a man's paycheck.
The teller called him Jared
and told him he needed a shower
which he admitted
he was headed toward.
He'd been on the boat since dawn
and had fallen into Tuckahoe River.
Unmistakably,
he smelled of trout,
the bucket of trout
my father and I caught
even though I didn't catch a thing.
How Dad expected a ten-year-old
like me to concentrate,
to watch the bobber
is a mystery.
My mind meandered around
every place I'd rather have been.
Woolworth's on Saturday,
shopping with the dollar
Poppop gave me every Friday.
Batting a tennis ball clumsily
with a racket missing strings
against the garage door,
brown paint chips flying
with every smack.
Playing Depth Charge with Scott Parker
in the Folsom Country Store
for however long
the quarters lasted.

Listening to Dad and his trumpet,
sitting on the threadbare carpeted steps
in the hallway,
as he played along to Herb Alpert on 8-track.
Meticulously, page by page,
scouring every inch of
the Johnson Smith catalog
and circling every single thing I wanted
before Dad yanked the rod and reel from my tiny arms.
I saw the rainbow
as he raised the fish over our heads
and spun him onto land.
"You almost lost it!" he accused
as he cut the line
and tossed the trout
into the bucket
with a splut.
That's when I smelled the boy.

Young Jimmy

Young Jimmy joins the swim team,
post eighth grade graduation.
Summer meets, scrimmages, practice.
Back stroke, curved spine.
Breast stroke, approaching manhood.
Butterfly, push, pull, recovery.
Front crawl, catching water.
Eyes sting, skin burns.
Jimmy dolphins end to end,
smooth, sublime.
He struts in Speedos to the locker room,
already naked and into the shower.
Cleansing stream, head to toes touching tile.
Soaps up, arching back,
young merman in his element
finally.

For Joseph

I take a walk through soft dirt, barefooted,
behind my house, behind the cheerless life
I've lived since I and Mother found you dead.
You left ten years' sobriety, a wife,
and me. My footprints echo all this weight
I've carried. Over countless dusks and dawns,
my footprints stiffen, fossilize, create
a record lasting long after I've gone.

Across the universe, magnificent beings
project themselves onto our planet Earth.
They bow their virtual heads in awe of seeing
my footprints, endless centuries past their birth.
Examining each step within that trail,
they read you in them easily, as Braille.

Welshie

The party is in a gallery
that used to be a barn.
I know no one except Jill,
who is busy hosting.
Her only advice: "You have to push you way to the wine."
I do.
It doesn't help,
my socially awkward self alone in a room full of artists
like but unlike myself.
They chat, laugh, flirt.
Acoustic musicians play popular tunes.
Hors d'oeuvres are consumed.
Without my husband,
who loves people but hates gatherings,
my attempted mingling fails
so I step outside the open barn door
into the brisk spring eve.
A man stands in front of me, soaking in the lush garden,
brilliant green trees darkening in the dusk.
He isn't my type,
clearly half my age,
but he's beautiful and blond.
He shakes my hand with ease.
"Ben."
"Bob. How do you know Jill?"
And we're off.

He's local for a bit,
brought to Jill's by a mutual.
America is new to him,
and though he'd planned to summer
here at the southern New Jersey shore,
he'll soon jet to Mexico,
which he's yet to see,

for some physical labor
and gallons of Tequila.
His passport is getting worn, he jokes,
and he talks of writing travelogue.
His grand idea of nomadic emigration
feeds his journaling,
the craft he's perfecting
seeing the world while
sleeping in hostels
or on borrowed couches
in exchange for some service or other
(not the sexy kind).
At his age,
I'd not seen more than a handful of states
and those usually involved
some sort of Six Flags.
I'm awed at his drive.

His Welshie accent echoes into my own past,
one bit of family history
about which the grands didn't lie.
And he listens respectfully
when I blather on
about getting back my mojo
and working in form
after black years and depression
bound my writing hand,
left me stuttering, struggling for words.
Even as we speak,
I'm already writing in my head
the final couplet of a sonnet about his eyes.
(Yes, blue. So blue.)
He's glad I'm cookin' again
and looks forward to reading my work.
We trade emails
and stand quiet in the night for a moment.

But his flip-flop toes are cold
so we step inside for more wine.
The party thinned out,
Jill and I reconnect.
Ben says goodbye,
shakes my hand again,
not knowing how much
he shook my status quo

Another Superman

He took my hand so gently, carefully,
he must have thought he'd crush it otherwise.
My heart was surely crying to be free
from his Kryptonian grip (and other ties
I'd rather not discuss). He laid me down
to prove the man was truly made of steel.
It filled the other Loises in town
with jealousy that Clark chose me, to feel.
But then I turned away, convinced he'd beg
for digits, dates, some other sacrifice.
I bid him go. So, cape between his legs,
he headed to his fortress in the ice.
Although I told that Superman goodbye,
the villain in me only wonders why.

Adrift

I was barely ten
the morning I climbed aboard a boat
that wasn't good for anything but getting lost.
Dad, who reckoned himself an angler,
rented Faithful Friend
and took his family fishing on Delaware Bay,
Labor Day Weekend, 1980.
My mother donned her bucket hat
and stowed a carpet bag filled with Harlequins
to pass her time.
My brother, future valedictorian,
brought a Nothing book with a Rolling Writer
to document his dreadful voyage.
I wasn't allowed to bring a thing.

The rough seas left my stomach
back on the dock (or I wished it so)
as we departed Port Norris.
Chilly morning clouds surrendered
to torrid afternoon sun
and fish that just weren't biting.
And when a huge weakie slipped my line
as I stared blankly at the horizon,
Dad got so mad I thought he would spit.
The hoagies were gone
by the time we were out of gas
somewhere south of Fenwick Island.
My mother drank the last can of Shop Rite cola.
We drifted,
trying to pass the time with twenty questions,
but my brother quit on round four
when I guessed Esther Williams in five.

Near dusk, the Coast Guard finally found us.
As the Dependable, giant and sturdy,
pulled alongside,
a huge man in a uniform dropped into the boat,
hoisted my boy's body easily,
thrusting me over his head toward the deck.
I felt two hands, strong and comfortable,
surround my chest and pull me up.
"That's it, Skipper,"
said this other huge man,
lines all over his smiling, ruddy face.
He kept his arm around me the whole way home.

I know my family was rescued as well,
but I don't remember it.

(Untitled)

My birthday found me 41,
and rather than standing at the bathroom mirror
pulling the skin back on my face,
I took a fist to it.
(The mirror…)
It smashed through the wall behind
into a black opening,
a space that didn't make sense.
I reached between the jagged glass
and felt the emptiness as warmth.
Nothing came into my grasp,
not rusted nails or splintered wood,
not creosote or fiberglass.
Withdrawing my hand,
I found it smooth,
soft,
perfect,
young.
I inserted the other hand
into the black,
pulled it back.
Young again,
corrected from the accident as well.
No deformed bone,
no surgery scars,
no crooked fingers.
I had to look in,
plucked the glass away gingerly
and laid it in the wastebasket.
Climbed up on the sink,
pushed in my head face first,
felt the same warm as before.
I couldn't see anything in that space
but didn't care.

I liked it.
It brought to mind
a memory from the womb,
of youth before understanding,
and I had a need to crawl in
as if I should have never left.
So I did.
But it turns out,
I just crawled into the wall.

Robert A. Geise has a Bachelor of Arts in Literature from Stockton University. Born and raised in southern New Jersey, he garnered a reputation as a notable gay poet in the Arts and Poetry community there. Robert has also appeared in several short films directed by Chris M. LaBree of 2255 Productions. Despite actively writing and honing his craft for more than twenty years, *Renting Superman* is the first collection of his work. Robert currently lives in Florida with his family.

www.ingramcontent.com/pod-product-compliance
Lightning Source LLC
Chambersburg PA
CBHW030252270626
47156CB00021B/1747